100 Word Horrors

Book 4

100 Word Horrors: Book 4 © 2019 Kevin J. Kennedy

Edited by Kevin J. Kennedy

Cover design by Michael Bray

First Printing, 2019

Other Books by KJK Publishing

Anthologies

Collected Christmas Horror Shorts
Collected Easter Horror Shorts
Collected Halloween Horror Shorts
Collected Christmas Horror Shorts 2
The Horror Collection: Gold Edition
The Horror Collection: Black Edition
The Horror Collection: Purple Edition
The Horror Collection: White Edition
100 Word Horrors
100 Word Horrors: Part 2
100 Word Horrors: Book 3
Carnival of Horror

Novels and Novellas

Pandemonium by J.C. Michael
You Only Get One Shot by Kevin J. Kennedy &
J.C. Michael
Screechers by Kevin J. Kennedy & Christina
Bergling

Collections

Dark Thoughts

Vampiro and Other Strange Tales of the Macabre

Foreword

I never know how to start these things, so I'll keep it short. If you have made it to book four of the 100 Word Horrors series, you already know I am a big fan of drabbles. While I enjoy the drabble format this will be the last book in the series, or at least for quite some time. There are a few reasons for this. The drabble anthologies are more work to put together than the normal type of anthology that I do, and while they are reasonably popular, other anthologies with longer stories sell better.

I suppose drabbles aren't for everyone. I'm always working on multiple projects at a time and I feel my energies would be better focussed in other places. The other reason for taking a break from the drabble anthos is the market is absolutely flooded with them right now. It means if I want to write a few drabbles, I have plenty of options of where to send them and it's a lot quicker than putting a whole book together. My first series of anthologies, the Collected Horror Shorts books, finished after four books so this seems like a good place to wrap things up.

Thank you for picking up a copy of this book and the others, if you did. I may revisit some of the series I've put together further down the line but for now I am only going to continue with the Collected Horror Shorts books and work on some other projects.

I hope you enjoy the 100 Word Horrors last hurrah!

Kevin J. Kennedy
Editor

Acknowledgements

I'd like to thank my pre readers, Darren Tarditi and Ann Keeran. I'd also like to thank Michael Bray for consistently providing me with fantastic covers for the series. Thanks to everyone who picked up the book and for all the support that readers have given KJK Publishing since I started three years ago. Without all of you, none of this would be possible. I'd like to say thanks to Brandy Yassa and Becky Narron for their support on previous books I've put together, and to everyone else who has stepped in and helped me out when I have needed it.

A final thanks to the authors who keep me loving books. There is something special about a book. I've been addicted to them since I have been young, and even today, I buy way more than I will ever be able to read. I now know how hard it is to work in this industry and the struggles that comes with finishing a longer piece of fiction. You guys amaze me and keep me involved. Without my love of reading, I wouldn't do what I do, so once again, thank you.

Extra-Curricular Clone

By
N.M. Brown

My daughter Shannon hates when I'm late to pick her up after school; which I am today.

Thankfully, she smiles at me when I arrive.

"How was school today honey?" I ask.

Crunching and slurping sounds resonate from the backseat.

"It was good!" She responds joyfully through chews.

My phone rings; it's Shannon's school.

"Mrs. Johnson, Shannon's been waiting here for half an hour. Are you coming? She's distraught. It's been a rough day for them today; the class hamster went missing."

The girl in the backseat giggles at me as I drop the phone.

Water World
By
Ann Christine Tabaka

The temperatures kept rising and rising. Nothing could be done to stop it now. The ice caps were already melting. As the sea levels rose, the coastal cities started to submerge under the oceans. The rivers and streams overflowed their banks. The farm land and forests were enveloped by the water. People climbed to higher ground, leaving all belongings behind. They were desperate to find safety.

This time there would be no rainbows as a promise, for man had brought the destruction upon himself. And the earth was now truly "the blue planet." A water world void of all humankind.

Swamplands
By
Paul D. Brazill

Elvis awoke in a cold, dank sweat, hungover from bourbon and bad dreams. The nightmares had consisted of him being hunted through a swamp by the murderous spectre of Jesse, his stillborn twin. His pounding heartbeat seemed to echo throughout the mansion. He stumbled into the bathroom, splashed cold water on his face and looked in the mirror, only to be confronted by his own ashen reflection and that of his grinning doppelganger. Jesse tightly wrapped the umbilical cord around Elvis' throat and pulled it until Elvis breathed no more. The king is dead, long live the king, he muttered.

Choke
By
Lee Mountford

I am restrained. A knife cuts a length of meat from my thigh. The woman wielding it takes a bite.

'You shouldn't have come looking for her,' she tells me as she chews my flesh. The her being referred to was my wife. A woman I can't live without. 'Bet you never imagined this is what happened to her? Eaten alive. Just like you are going to be...'

But, you see, I did know. I figured it all out. And I poisoned myself before being caught. The toxin will soon be in this woman's bloodstream, too.

Choke on me, bitch!

Eternal Life
By
Ross Baxter

Thinking about the old days usually perked him up, especially when he remembered his steadfast and uncompromising thirst for knowledge. It was the trait which eventually led him to devote all his time, money and effort into trying to discover the secret for eternal life.

Despite the cost, the hours and the setbacks, his eureka moment finally did come, and he achieved the knowledge he so desperately craved. But laying helplessly alone in his soiled bed on the eve of his two hundredth birthday, rotting but unable to ever die, he readily acknowledged that some secrets were better left undiscovered.

Mister Mushroom
By
Joel R Hunt

There was a man at the end of the lane who they called Mister Mushroom. His shabby brown coat smelled of damp. His slippers left wet stains wherever he walked. His face, what little of it could be seen beneath his battered hat, was mottled and pale. There was something growing on Mister Mushroom's skin; that's what the children said.

On his trips to the market, pieces would fall off of Mister Mushroom. Tiny, sponge-like scabs that clung to people's shoes. To their clothes.

To their skin.

Now they have a new name for Mister Mushroom.

They call him "Father".

Chiaroscuro Morning
By
Kevin Wetmore

"Daddy!"

Steve opened his eyes to see his three-year-old daughter's face two inches from his. He glanced at the clock on the nightstand.

"It's six in the morning, sweetie. What is it?"

"There's a shadow in my room!"

"Turn on a light, Sophie, then the shadow will go away."

"I did, daddy."

"Problem solved, honey. Go back to sleep."

He heard her scamper back down the hall to her room and fell back asleep.

"Daddy?"

He sighed and opened his eyes. "Yes, honey?"

"The shadow would like to talk to you."

Behind her the darkness grew darker and moved closer.

Road Kill
By
Dawn DeBraal

Three desperate men and a boy hunkered down on the roadside, waiting for someone to come by. It had been many days since they'd seen anyone come. They were starving. It had been almost a week since they had eaten something. Strange how all the leaves had fallen from the trees. Even though it was June, it looked like late fall. The radiation that caused the leaves to fall was also rotting the skin from their bodies. Rags were used to protect open wounds. They waited because there was nothing else, they could do. The boy started to look tasty.

The Wave
By
Andrew Lennon

Every night since I was a kid, I'd wake and look out the window to the back garden, there he was.

A tall black shadow, just standing there, waving slowly at my window. I sometimes consider waving back, but I get scared, shut the windows and hurry back to bed, praying that it's just a dream.

Tonight though, I couldn't resist the urge. I waved.

The man vanished. Suddenly I hear crashing from behind as the large shadow storms towards me.

"Why?" I screamed.

"Because you can see me, my friend," came the whisper just before the darkness consumed me.

Better Off Dead
By
Zoey Xolton

Standing on the precipice, black eyes swollen, arms cut from fending off the knives once more, Lilith teetered. Below the sea sung to her—calling her by name. There was a place down there on the rocks for her. Perhaps the sirens of old would claim her, wash away her hurts and eat her broken soul?

Holding her baby against her chest, she wept. She couldn't let her daughter grow up with that monster. It would be a fate crueller than death.

"I love you," she whispered, kissing Persephone's forehead. "I'm so sorry."

Together they fell...but the rocks caught them.

The Children of Earth
By
Ann Christine Tabaka

They seemed to come out of nowhere, unnoticed at first, so small they were barely detectable. As they started to grow, they took the form of pods. They became larger, resembling brown baseballs, and finally the size of basketballs. The globes continued to expand until they were everywhere. One by one they started to terraform until they looked like miniature green planets.

The Earth started to crumble and shrink. People panicked, not knowing what to do. The Earth was dying, and in her last breaths, she spawned the next generation of worlds. And so were born the Children of Earth.

Swing Low
By
Evans Light

"Swing low, sweet chariot, coming for to carry me home..."

The farmhouse shrunk in the distance as the massive man traversed a field thick with wildflowers.

The screams felt close, but the woodline still seemed so far away.

Fresh blood spiraled down his arm onto the axe handle as he sang.

"I looked over Jordan and what did I see, coming for to carry me home? A band of angels coming after me..."

The steel blade bumped along the ground, still unclean despite trampled flowers brushing underneath, delicate white petals now streaked with red.

"Coming for to carry me home."

The Golden Sticker
By
David Owain Hughes

Timmy's eyes bugged. "The last sticker needed to complete my Marvellous Monsters and Madmen album!" He let the sticker's wrapper drop. "Finally, after months of searching!"

The book, bought by his dad at The World's Mysteries shop, lay on his bed.

"Don't tell Mum!" Dad had warned.

Timmy flipped the pages and found the empty slot. Around the blank space were stickers depicting horror legends and Universal Monsters.

Timmy ripped the back off the sticker and smoothed it into place.

"Fin—"

The album flew across the room, landing by the bed, the icons emerging from within with growling satisfaction.

Livestock
By
RJ Meldrum

"Those five," said Stan to the ranch-hands, pointing.

Hank, standing beside him at the fence, stared out at the pen. He was new, two weeks into the job. The sight still amazed him.

"I can't believe it. The plague was meant to have died out before I was born."

"It did, but we kept two as breed stock."

"And the customers don't know?"

"It's marketed as dry-aged beef."

"Where do you get them?"

"Hikers, campers, hitchhikers. Once they're here, we infect them. Six weeks later the flesh is aged to perfection."

Hank stared out at the milling zombies.

"Just amazing."

Molly's Wedding
By
Julian J. Guignard

Molly got engaged, and, for a year, planned her perfect wedding at a mountain resort.

A week before the event, she was hanging decorations outside when she fell over a ledge. She got up, not allowing a dumb fall to ruin her wedding plans.

The wedding day came, and it was perfect as planned. Molly received a giant gold-and-diamond ring, and everyone applauded.

Afterward, she suddenly looked puzzled and walked away.

Her husband chased after and found her under a ledge, dead and decomposed for a week.

But she wore the gold-and-diamond ring he'd just given for her perfect wedding.

Zombie
By
Jackk N. Killington

Things crawled on him, biting him. He felt them in his skin, burrowing deep. He tried to draw breath, but no breath came. Earth surrounded him, he started to move. Slowly at first as his body learned again. The earth softened, became pliable. Dig. Dig upwards. Through the rocks, and dirt that had held him for time unknown. Soon he broke through, though he did not taste the air. He took a look at his surroundings while he pulled himself out of his make shift crypt. Hearing voices somewhere, he felt a hunger welling within. Moving with one thought: feed.

Every Fifty Years the Roots Need Blood
By
Ellen A. Easton

Dear girl, come down to the woods to play.
The day grows dark and the heavens turn
gray.
She hides under trees as the rain bites down,
Long prickly branches slash her face and
gown.
Please come home, her parents shout in
fright,
And she whimpers as the forest fills with
jagged light.
The crash of thunder roars through the sky,
And the shadows surround her when she
starts to cry.
A sharp, sudden scream pierces the night
Followed by silence; the stars come alight.
The forest's hunger is again appeased
And her bloody bones sway gently in the
breeze.

Revived
By
Dawn DeBraal

Edgar held her head underwater until the last bubbles left her. Charlotte's vacant eyes stared back at him through the clear water. There was beauty in her death. She looked like a china doll with blue lips and white skin. He regretted that he had gone too far this time in his attempt to scare her. He couldn't take it back. Pulling her from the water, he administered CPR. Coughing, Charlotte came back to life. Edgar's excitement grew. He'd brought her back from the dead. How many times could he do this? Poor Charlotte, he was excited to find out.

No Time Like the Present
By
Adam Light

The clock ticked like a hammer blow to the center of her forehead. She gasped, checked her watch. No time like the present.

The clock ticked again, shaking her brain around within her skull. Indecision was apt to polarize her if she did not act quickly, and so she walked into the kitchen.

The music was loud, intolerably so; it was the song she despised the most. She could have let him keep washing the dishes, and the day would have continued like any other.

Instead, she swung the knife in a violent downward arc, slamming it into his back.

A Prison Inside Us
By
Sheldon Woodbury

I've discovered there's a hideous place inside us where we lock away what we fear the most, a psychic prison that's not part of our flesh and blood. It's a mind shattering slaughterhouse where everything we love is defiled and destroyed. I'm telling you this because I was dragged there in my nightmares and the worst part of me has now escaped. I'm begging you with all my heart to please forgive me. The strange gurgling sound you hear in the dark is next to you. I'm waiting for you to wake up and see the glorious monster I've become.

To Feed A Monster
By
Terry Miller

Before the virus changed her, Val had me chain her to the chair. She wanted me to kill her if she became one of them but I couldn't. Each day I bring her some reject off the street.

It was fine at first but my conscience has been ailing me. Val is dead, this is some monster wearing her rotting face.

As long as I'm alive, I'll feed it. I can't fight these tears but I got to do what I got to do. I reach out and its teeth sink into my arm. This is where I say goodbye.

Lanterns
By
Simon Cluett

The wheelbarrow's intermittent squeak punctuated the darkness like the mewl of an angry cat. A squirt of WD40 should do the trick.

Another bloody chore on the 'To Do' list.

They'd been on at him to carve Jack O' Lanterns. He'd buckled, inevitably, victim to their incessant whining. Now the deed was done he could enjoy some peace and quiet.

Finally.

He'd severed their heads with a sturdy hacksaw. Scooping out the mess like dollops of cherry ice cream. He glanced down at the barrow. Three hollow skulls stared back.

He couldn't wait to see their little faces light up.

The Guest Room
By
Jack Lothian

The door to the guest room wouldn't stay shut. She'd close it and walk away, but by the time she'd glanced back, it'd be open again. Walking backward, eyes fixed on it, made no difference; she'd blink, and it'd be ajar. Hammering it closed led to twisted metal nails scattered across the carpet by dawn.

The landlord shrugged, said it was an old house.

One night she tried closing the door from inside the room. It clicked shut and then refused to open. She was trapped.

As the lights flickered out, she discovered just how old the house really was.

Wrath of the Old Ones
By
Kevin J. Kennedy

The gods never disappeared, they were always here. They had just become bored of us and stopped paying attention. They watched other planets as they evolved with renewed curiosity, but when they checked in on us again, they felt only disappointment. In old texts, everything happens on a massive scale and the gods live in the sky. The reality is less grand. You turn on your TV and you see murders, rape, genocide, war, famine and many other atrocities. This is not the will of man. This is the old gods, walking among us once again and showing their wrath.

My Brother Gets Released Today
By
Tristan Drue Rogers

There was this cool tarantula that lived in the light fixtures of my bedroom. When my brother walked in, interrupting our conversation, the tarantula with the red Converse high-tops climbed into his ear, making him go insane.

I told him, "If it's not taken out, he'd stay crazy."

He was always the crazy one, for sure.

So we dug it out of his ear. For a while, my brother helped.

Soon enough, I was doing all the work.

The tarantula, who lost its shoes, told me that he was going to jail anyway.

He was the crazy one after all.

35

A Shape in the Dark
By
Jason Parent

I don't know what we're fighting. I just know we're dying.

Breaths come short and fast. Fingers fumble with powder and ball as I load my musket. The enemy's banshee wails have many shaken. Men flee the front, but our captain orders them back. Refusers are executed. Every path leads to death.

A horn blows, and I break cover. The march is on.

The field is overrun. A shape in the dark races towards me. I fire and miss. Still, it comes, shrieking and hissing.

As I stab it with my bayonet, I see its face. It looks like mine.

The Coffin
By
Kevin Cathy

My scream sounds so localized.

I grab my lighter from my pants and light it.

There are only inches of space between me and the surrounding wood.

How did I get here?

I don't remember much, but I do know what the inside of a coffin looks like... and now feels like.

I try to push the top; it doesn't budge.

I see a red orange light materializing beneath me.

I squint to make out what the light resembles. I frown. I realize what it is.

The bottom of the coffin releases me and I quickly descend into the fire.

Louie's Room
By
C.M. Saunders

Our six-year old son Louie loves playing with soldiers. He arranges his battalions of plastic armies in perfect formations, recreating battles and skirmishes. He gets carried away sometimes and, despite our parental posturing, insists on staying up far too late. We can hear him right now in his room above us. The unmistakeable sounds of a fake war being played out on the carpet. The 'booms' and 'arghs,' and the rat-tat-tat of mimicked machine gun fire. It's somehow comforting to listen to. Even though they couldn't remove the cancer and he didn't survive the operation, Louie still loves to play.

Mine
By
Nerisha Kemraj

Joanne stood paralyzed with fear. Goosebumps lined her skin as an icy finger traced the side of her neck. He moved silently in the dark. Her nerves screamed for her to run but she couldn't move. Her heart thundered, threatening to explode.

The familiar cologne broke Joanne's frozen spell.

"What do you want, Derek?"

He laughed.

"You. Always you."

A knife glinted in his hands.

She turned to run but strong arms grabbed her into an inescapable grip. She was trapped.

"Your heart belongs to me. Not him. I'm here to take what's mine."

The chloroform welcomed her into darkness.

The Theatre of Screams
By
Howard Carlyle

James had been given some medication, he was conscious, but unable to move. A nurse said it was time to go theatre where the doctor was waiting for him.

James didn't know why, or even how, he got there.

The nurse pushed his bed along a corridor and through some double doors, where the doctor was waiting with a scalpel in his hand.

James could hear people chattering, before noticing a huge pair of curtains open up before him.

"Gentlemen, who will start the bidding on the subject's lungs?"

This was not the type of theatre that James had imagined.

Worth It
By
Matthew A Clarke

Tick. Tick. Tick. Tick.

I watch the timer intently while struggling against my bonds. Fifty-six. Fifty-five. I never thought my life would end like this, in my head it had been a flawless plan. Muted noises from outside my dark cage, people trying to break in?

With each passing second the curved blade swings closer to my throat.

I close my eyes and pray to a god I never believed in. How was I supposed to know she was the daughter of a madman? I just wanted to see what it felt like to take a life.

Still worth it.

Blood in the Moonlight
By
Robin Braid

I wiped down the axe with my shredded shirt, then leant it against the open door of the woodshed and paused for breath. Sunrise still felt a long way off.

Under the cold moonlight, I dragged the bloody sack outside, emptied it onto the hard ground, and placed the heads in a row, eyes agape and fangs bared. A welcome party for the next wave.

A large shadow passed over the face of the moon, momentarily blacking out the light. They were coming, in greater numbers this time. I lifted the axe onto my shoulder and roared into the darkness.

Feeding the Beast
By
Lee Franklin

Screams of terror and the crashing grind of metal on metal is deafening as the selected few are shot forward into the ravenous maw of the beast. An abyss of darkness that reeks of fear tainted with vomit awaits us as we shuffle forward like cattle in our lines. The beast releases a gentle sigh of contentment as it casts off its waste into the chaos below. I search amongst the thick press of bodies for a way to escape. I'm trapped and pushed forward. My hands are clammy as I climb into the rollercoaster. What we do for thrills.

A Friend for Ellie
By
P.J. Blakey-Novis

I only got the Ouija board out when I'd had a few drinks. I'd used it twice without result. The third time's the charm, so they say. Now my precious daughter, Ellie, is no longer lonely. She has a best friend who is always with her, or within her may be more accurate. I can't say I like the way she/they look at me sometimes, the unblinking stares and crooked grin, especially when I wake to find Ellie standing over me. My daughter wouldn't hurt me. I'm not so sure about her friend but at least she isn't lonely now.

Cattle
By
Ryan Colley

You ever go down one of those internet rabbit holes, where you keep clicking and can't remember where you started? I used to do that.

One day, I ended up on a buried forum where the posters spoke about buying cattle – there was a link that I curiously clicked.

I'll never forget those girls faces. Each and every one of them, bound and gagged, beaten and crying. I definitely won't forget the anonymous users in chat discussing them like meat. One asked why they were so cheap.

The host replied, "Cattle is easy to find and no one'll miss them."

Open Call
By
Steve Stred

"I said I wouldn't do this again," the editor posted," but I'm doing another open call."

Email after email, the stories kept flooding in. Kevin sat in awe at just how talented the submissions were. He grinned and grimaced as characters were killed and heroes were vanquished.

This was his fourth anthology of 100 Word Horrors and he thought it would be the best.

The final email popped up – a sender he didn't recognize.

Opening it, he was horrified.

Photo after photo showing his demise.

A noise startled him from behind.

Turning, he saw a dark figure holding a camera.

The Job Interview
By
Ron Davis

"Thank you for seeing me today, Mr...."

"No problem Samuels. The position that you inquired about is still available, if you have what it takes."

"Yes sir, I believe that I do."

"Can you be ruthless?"

"Yes sir."

"Cutthroat?"

"Yes sir."

"Willing to trample anyone who gets in your way?"

"Yes sir."

"Good. We are a very competitive company. We value discretion and failure will not be tolerated. Is that understood Samuels?"

"Yes sir."

"Prove it. Here is your weapon and the name of your first target. We expect him to be dispatched within the hour. No witnesses."

"Yes sir!"

The Transylvania Box
By
Joel R Hunt

"I know your grandfather was a monster hunter, but did he have to keep all these grisly trophies?"

"It's a Van Helsing tradition. Now, Dracula's amulet should be around here somewhere. Check that box marked 'Transylvania'."

Giles reached inside, but flinched as a sharp pain bit into his finger. The box fell, spilling its contents over the floor.

A cape. Rosary beads. Two long, yellowing fangs.

"Are you alright?" Amelia asked.

"Fine."

Giles sucked his bleeding finger. It tasted... sweet.

As Amelia knelt down to look for the amulet, her hair fell aside, revealing her neck.

Her slender, blood-filled neck.

Hide and Seek
By
Eddie D. Moore

Kenny repositioned the phone on the table again and glanced at the detective. "Detective Mann, thanks for staying with me. You haven't left my side since I reported her missing. It's been almost two days; I'm sure your family misses you."

The detective nodded. "They understand."

After taking a deep breath, Kenny asked, "Is it true that the odds of finding her drop after forty-eight hours?"

"We're going to do our best to find her. I promise."

Kenny glanced at the tiles under the detective's chair and cleaned the last of the concrete and grouting out from under his fingernails.

Inescapable End
By
Micah Castle

Twisting, ash spires rose from the soot blanketed ground. The deep gray overcast loomed over the dead world. He stepped lightly through the long deceased. Ahead the ash gave way to earth, revealing crude umber stone stairs, jutting from sleek, colorless walls. He carefully took them, one step after another. At the bottom was absolute darkness, and he inhaled the gloom and exhaled it out from the well. The darkness gone, a group of huddling men and women appeared. Bruised, beaten, hollow. He stepped before them and put out his hand. They had no choice; Death could not be ignored.

Vulture
By
Veronica Smith

I'm gliding on the wind, looking for my next meal. Is that the smell of blood in the air; the smell of rot? Swooping lower for a closer look, I see it. It's a deer, already dead. No waiting around this time, I can eat right away. Stupid animal probably stopped in front of one of those big metal things as it crossed the smooth, hard earth. It's laying there on the grass; Mother Nature's platter. I drop to the ground beside the feast. Friends are flying overhead and they are welcome to share as long as they aren't greedy.

Books-A-Million
By
David Owain Hughes

Maximillian didn't consider collecting books as hording. "It's not hording if it's books," he'd tell his wife.

"I hope you have literature on coping with divorce," she'd said, slamming the front door.

Books from thrift shops and the like stood in ceiling-reaching stacks on an insurmountable number of shelves around his living space, blocking out both natural and synthetic light.

I don't care, he thought, stroking a pile. Only de—

A shelf creaked; a board broke. An avalanche of black and white crashed down on Max, crushing him. A copy of Until Death Do Us Part lay by his side.

Hair
By
Timothy Friesenhahn

Waking up sweating profusely, Kyla felt extreme pressure in her belly button. Using her phone light, she looked at her navel. With utter shock and disgust, she saw a wad of hair poking from her belly buttonhole. The wad of hair twitched and caused her to sweat even more. From her stomach she felt the urge to vomit. Standing in her bathroom she took tweezers to the wad of hair. As she pulled the wad out, she realized it kept coming out until a two-foot-long fuzzy worm fell to the floor full of blood. In extreme pain, she passed out.

Stop
By
Mark Steensland

Stop! Don't read another word of this. Oh, no. Too late. Why don't you people ever listen to me? Now you can't stop because he is behind you. Your reading these words has brought him forth. Don't look at him! Don't even breathe. If you do, he will be able to take you away and then you'll be beyond my help forever. If you want to live, keep your eyes right here and do exactly as I say. There are only two words that can stop him now. You must read them before he reaches you. They are

The End

Meal
By
John Boden

Grandpa licks wrinkled lips and Grandma smiles.

Brother and Sister and I sit with our knives and forks clutched in small sweating hands.

Papa sits at the head of the table, napkin tucked into the collar of his shirt.

Mama comes in, looking tired and struggling to carry the large serving tray.

The metal oval clangs when she sits it on the table and she wipes her hands on her apron.

She lifts the silver lid and everyone smiles and oohs and ahhs.

Papa picks up the knife and stoops to start carving. He frowns.

"You left the diaper on."

Sanatorium
By
Constanze Scheib

You heard them rustling under the floorboards. The nurse didn't believe you.

At night you felt them climbing onto your bed. You didn't dare move as they crawled on your face. Their little mouths nibbling, not biting, to experience your taste.

The next morning the doctor thought you were crazy. He shook his head sadly and gave you more pills to relax you.

It got dark and they returned. Bigger and fiercer, their stench was unbearable, their bodies were wet. Your scream died in your throat, as they took large chunks out of your flesh.

Tomorrow they would believe you.

The Hunter
By
Darren Tarditi

6 weeks I've been watching and waiting.

3am, quick lock pick on the flimsy back door. Wait and listen, silence.

Creep up the stairs, skipping the creaky 4th I'd found the previous week.

Straight in the room, the streetlight shining in the window just glinting on the edge of the massive blade before I plunged it straight into the chest.

Silent scream for about 2 seconds then life leaves the body.

Remove the blade quick and go straight in for a fresh bloody feast, there's nothing like the taste of warm blood from a fresh kill.

Armageddon
By
Theresa Jacobs

Sweet sickly rot perfumes the air. Grunts, moans, and screams replace horns, sirens, and our old familiarity. Cars no longer have room to maneuver as lumbering hoards meander the streets. People are forced to hide behind boarded up doors and windows.

Daylight rarely seen.

While the dead writhe in angst-ridden freedom.

The end came, not on climate's violent wings, but in the teeth of the virus stricken. The hunger of the gnashing, unsympathetic dead—never sated. Our world is lost to us, as we fight a never-ending battle.

Death is no longer the end. But a new way of life.

Dark Legion
By
Toneye Eyenot

The guts of the earth are torn open, spitting forth an incomprehensible force. Dimension disruption that staggers the mind, a summoning bred from pure malice and hate.

Metal rends flesh, stone crushes bone, wood-splintered skulls still screaming. Two worlds become one, a nightmare hell-zone – wide awake, humanity thrown into dreaming.

Man's horrified spirit broken, food for the legion who make their new home. Demonic enslavement, the end of mankind – ancient evil atop the food chain.

Fresh human flesh torn from bone. Bloodied fangs in the night, gleaming. Two worlds now one, a nightmare hell-zone...

The sound of seven-billion souls screaming

The Hunter
By
Alanna Robertson-Webb

My woodland walks have become a nightmare. I used to love hiking through the uninhabited forest behind my house, my dog Rex at my side and a lunch in my backpack, but not now.

Last month mutilated animal carcasses began appearing on my property, and each day we find them closer to the house. Rex growls at night sometimes, and I swear I've heard my doorknob jiggle.

This morning a note, scrawled in childish handwriting, was written on my door in blood.

U r next

Rex has been barking constantly since sunset, and I've never feared the dark so much.

My Sincerest Apologies to Any Innocent Victims
By
Billy San Juan

You know who you are.

You left me at the altar. I wept for years. Well, I finally have my revenge. It was convoluted. It took some time. But I know how much you love horror stories. I knew you would read this book. You always loved reading this "horror" crap. So, I bought a plane ticket. Snuck into the printing press. Tampered with some things. And now I have my revenge. Now you'll regret the pain you've caused. Because I know you lick your finger when turning the page. And the pages in this book are coated with arsenic.

Blood and Bone
By
Stacey Jaine McIntosh

There are years scattered among the bones, unused and forfeit. She gobbles them up in greedy handfuls.

"I knew what you were from the beginning. I could smell the blood. You were born to spill blood, child."

The child - a boy - smiles. "Maybe I was."

The old woman smiled a crooked smile. Once white teeth are now blackened with age.

He shrugged, his smile fading. "But I can't help how I was born."

"No, I don't suppose you can," the crone said. "But I can ensure you live up to your potential whether you like it or not."

Shingles on a graham-cracker roof
By
Chad Lutzke

Jed slid the file under his thumbnail. The sound was like skittering spiders on parchment as the nail pulled away. The frost-bitten digit felt nothing.

He placed the nail on the gingerbread house—a lone, blackened shingle on a graham-cracker roof. He eyed his other fingers.

Ten shingles on a graham-cracker roof.

He removed his socks, toes burning from December's bite.

Twenty shingles on a graham-cracker roof.

With no nails remaining, Jed frowned at the incomplete house, then smiled at the thought of those asleep above him. With file in hand, he headed upstairs.

Sixty shingles on a graham-cracker roof.

Panto Season
By
Joe X Young

"He's behind you!" They shouted at the stage. Aladdin strains forward, one hand to his ear to get the public to repeat the shout. They oblige, louder.

"He's behind you!" It's quite the ritual, 600 people watching a story told so often that there is never a surprise.

"He's behind you!" It's nice sometimes to be able to forget the rat race and to immerse yourself into something as simple as pantomime. But not tonight, as my show must go on.

"I'm behind you!" I whisper to the man in front of me as my straight razor ends his show.

Noisy Neighbours
By
Sue Oldham

It was the hammering that had got to him in the end. The endless pounding, thumping reverberations. It felt at times like the entire house was shaking. Thump, thump, thump; it was becoming too much to take.

He rose to his feet; enough was enough. Time to do something about it.

Wincing in pain, his headache worsening, he looked down; his arm was coated in blood, brain and gore to the elbow. Disgusted, he threw the hammer carelessly aside, reaching into his tool-box for the saw instead.

"This should be much quieter," he sighed, kneeling once more alongside the body.

Cats
By
Callum Pearce

Only cats can see them until they come for you. The demons follow us and watch our lives. So much better for creating just the right hell for us at the end. Everybody gets one. Nobody is without sin. Maybe you feel him, sense his hunger.

Perhaps your cat is watching you now, as you read these words. Or perhaps he is watching something else. Something leaning over you. Hot, foul, breath caressing your neck. Saliva dripping from his long, razor-sharp teeth. Wondering how you will taste at the end. Marinated in fear and sweat. Has the cat run yet?

Curiosity
By
Gary McDonough

The large gelatinous blob hit the floor with a loud splat! Thick goo splashed his new trainers. Mum would kill him! He'd only had them 3 days.

It took a moment to notice that the skin from his wrist down had slid from his body like a glove, leaving a skeletal hand pointing at the mess on the floor.

He shouldn't have opened the jar.

Pain travelled through his body.

Slipping in his own slop he fell to the ground.

His face began to leave his skull, jar still in sight, he thought, 'What did mum used to say, Curiosity...'

Missing Halloween
By
Kevin J. Kennedy

No one ever wanted to trick 'r treat with me. I wasn't popular, and the kids called me names. My mum wouldn't let me go out myself, so I missed it every year. Then when I was older, I was told I was too old to do it. It always looked so fun. Now though, I never miss a year. I get a new costume every time and go to different places. The kids still don't want to be my friend. No matter, I always catch them, kidnap them, then cook them. Halloween treats are as tasty as I imagined.

Hunger Pains
By
Chloe Lennon

He watched hungrily. It had been God knows how long since he last ate. His stomach grumbled impatiently. *'Just a few more minutes'*, he thought as the rabbit hopped through the field, oblivious. It would have been such a lovely evening, had the world not gone crazy. What had once been a blue ocean was red, either reflecting the post-apocalyptic sky or polluted with blood. He pounced on top of the poor rabbit and, not unlike a wolf, decapitated and ate it. He should've been disgusted, but this was life now, and in this world it's every man for himself.

Lair
By
Jacek Wilkos

He lay on the bed, waiting. When everybody fell asleep, he pulled up his shirt, revealing a long scar under his arm. Limbs flattened as if they were deflated and the torso bulged. Slender fingers slid out of the wound. Something slipped from the body onto the floor and crawled under the bed. The narrow, dark place imitated its natural lair.

In the morning it'll quickly slip into its shell and cover the wound with clothing. It is careful. It scrupulously hides the details distinguishing it from a human being. This can never come to light.

They all do so.

Awaken to Death
By
Tina Piney

I fumbled into consciousness confused by the absolute dark. My wounds were egregious, the pain was the only light I needed to see them by. I drank the moist air in gulps, but it didn't quench my body's need for oxygen.

I stopped, willing myself to calm, to assess my situation. My hands were my eyes feeling around the small space. The walls, the roof, the pillow beneath my head; satin. I'm in a coffin! I pushed the lid and shifted my weight around. It didn't budge. I've been buried! Scratching, screaming terror and then the dark swallowed me whole.

Bus Home
By
Russell Smeaton

The bus lurched out of the stop and chugged away. Wiping a porthole in the steamy window, I peered out over a sea of fog. Seeing nothing, I felt sleep steal over me.

Woken by the bus driver shouting incoherently, I staggered off the bus into a cool, clear night.

A friendly voice behind me said "Come, you'll have questions" and I looked back at what had been the bus. The front was now missing, replaced by the wreckage of 3 smashed cars. My body hung like a rag doll from a broken window.

I went with the friendly voice.

Misadventures of an Aggrieved Recluse
By
Eric J. Guignard

Shoes containing severed feet wash ashore the coasts of Canada's Salish Sea. It's claimed a natural occurrence of decomposition from people who commit suicide or die from "misadventure" along the cliffs and bridges bordering the harbors.

I like that name—Misadventure—for it's who I wish to be, an adventuress, and not this lonely old cripple, avenging herself on the cruel, the liars, the deviants, who mock me, hurt me...

I dream of that identity while luring another of them to my drowning traps and disposing of their bodies along the coasts of the Salish Sea...

Call me: Miss Adventure.

Haunted House
By
Cecelia Hopkins-Drewer

The girls screamed and clutched each other, while the hulking shape rose from the basement. The phantom was shrouded in black and moved soundlessly. Somewhere outside, an owl cried hoarsely, and the wooden walls creaked as the wind moaned through the rafters.

Their breathing sounded loud. Asthmatic Minta began to wheeze. The phantom hovered just in front of them.

"What do you want?" Carmine ventured.

The figure gestured wordlessly, forcing the girls to shuffle uncomfortably until they reached the trapdoor. There was no staircase. The ghost pointed downward, towards the pile of bones scattered across the stony subfloor.

"No…"

Motivation
By
Andrew Lennon

He makes me write. I don't even know why I do this. I'm not a writer. I'm supposed to be a model, that was until I ended up in this god damned cellar for so long. When was the last time I plucked my eyebrows? I don't know, it doesn't matter. I need to finish this story.

I glance to my side and see the reflection from the blade sticking out of his gut. The claret gives me inspiration, but not enough, I'm not a writer.

I'll leave soon, now that he's dead, but not until I finish this story.

Slaughter by the Full of the Moon
By
Toneye Eyenot

Our brothers and sisters are howling, calling us into the hills. Their eerie song invites us to join the hunt. Tonight, the town will be gutted, on unhallowed ground, bodies strewn.

Our hair turns outward, emergence of the beast within. Tooth to fang, nail to claw, our clothing torn, discarded. Our panting breath a manic rhythm. Our hearts pound as one to the beat of their doom.

In the foothills, we gather, the townsfolk tucked in their beds. Behind locked doors, their last prayers recited.

No locks or prayers will save them now. A hundred strong, we storm the town.

Predator
By
Lee Mountford

We'd spoken online for a while. He'd told me he was a fourteen-year-old boy, only one year older than me. I'd agreed to meet him. And now we were alone.

Isolated.

The fat, greasy man touched a wet tongue to his chapped lips.

'Oh, you are perfect, little girl.'

He started to loosen his belt. I smiled, too. The man gave a confused frown. But then he saw my teeth--fangs that grew longer. In the full moon, the transformation was quick.

'As are you,' I told him. His terrified screams were as delicious as his fatty flesh.

Grave Concerns
By
Zoey Xolton

The graveyard was silent and still as dusk descended. The moment the sun sunk beneath the hills, freshly dug earth and solid ground alike, stirred, and rasping voices rose. Pale hands burst through the soil, reaching skyward, and sunken flesh clawed its way out of the grave.

The groundsman reloaded his shotgun, sheathed knives and holstered his hatchet. He was getting on, and this game was growing old.

His apprentice, Jason, stood wide-eyed—frozen. "Rachel?" he whispered.

The groundsman took aim...moments later Rachel's decayed brains painted a nearby tree.

Jason's howl of anguish joined the cacophony of the living undead.

Summer Snow
By
RJ Meldrum

I remember it clearly. 1941. I was five. I was in the yard when the grey flakes started falling. I thought it was snow. I was excited to see snow in July. I only stopped when my mother screamed at me from the kitchen.

"Gretchen! Get inside immediately."

Her face was horrified as she thumped the dust from my clothes.

It wasn't till years later I understood why. It was only then I connected the flakes with the trains, the soldiers and the people in striped pajamas. It was only then I connected the flakes with the camp next door.

The Museum of Horrors
By
Sheldon Woodbury

There's a museum in Hell where the demons keep their worst atrocities, shrouded away for only the most wicked to see. It's where their most beastly cravings and brutal desires are collected in one blasphemous place. The crumbling front door is a bleeding hole of splattered bones and the burning walls are made from the wailing faces of tortured souls. It's hidden in the lowest depths of Hell in a crackling crater of ash, the sulphurous sanctuary where demons worship depravity. I'm telling you this because you need to know the next exhibition hanging on the walls will be you.

Diamond Lake Killer
By
Jack Lothian

The officers checked the dead man's cabin, found the machete, the mask, the bloodied overalls.

The suspect had seemed so normal, it was hard to believe he'd killed all those people.

They wondered what had made him act that way.

Back at the station Patrolman Brown tried on the mask.

"Look at me," he said. "I'm the Diamond Lake Killer."

The others laughed as he pantomimed stabbing the air.

"You can take it off now," said Sergeant Valdez.

But Brown just stood there, still making the slashing gestures, unable to hear them over the congregation of voices in his head.

Long Limbs at the E.R.
By
Tristan Drue Rogers

The patient's arm began excessively itching at home. She had tried allergy medicine to no avail. She tried having a neighbor watch her cat to see if the ailments would persist or not. Not long after, her pores around the reddened spot formed a large, pus-filled boil, which eventually sprouted a dozen ever moving spider-like legs, almost dancing, without distance.

Screaming in panic, as one should in such a situation, she ran into the street, in turn hitting a bus coming to a stop at the light. It was a miracle that she survived.

Her arm, however, was never recovered.

Inescapable
By
Kevin Cathy

It all began like any other chore.

I went looking for a shirt in the walk-in closet.

Suddenly, the door slams shut.

I don't live with anybody.

I try opening the door; it won't budge.

I try breaking it down. It's wood; it should break. It doesn't.

What the hell is going on!?

I begin to feel claustrophobic.

If this was your typical horror movie, this kind of situation would end with a monster killing me or me being able to open the door at some point.

Neither occurs.

Instead, I still sit here.

It's been days.

I'm beyond dehydrated.

Undead Champion
By
Robin Braid

Jack Shock was Heavyweight Champion. All tanned, toned muscle and bright, white teeth. He could annihilate any man, living or undead.

In those days they would just wire the mouths of the undead shut. Jack's favourite finish was to piledrive them headfirst into the mat, snapping their neck clean and sending the skull spinning into the side of the cage.

One day, the wire came loose and Jack's hand was bitten. By the time they got him out of there, he was too far gone.

Jack Shock is still Heavyweight Champion. All cold, pale muscle and bolted iron mouth guard.

You Look Prettier When You Smile
By
Lee Franklin

She stands in the line with her friend; eyes glazed staring at her phone. She would be pretty if she smiled. I can help her. Tonight I came for the different thrills of the carnival, but I'm always prepared and she needs my help. I sit behind her in the roller coaster and flick the piano string around her neck. The jolt and jerk of the ride saws the string through flesh and cartilage. Now she is smiling, her friend is screaming. We are all screaming it is a scary ride. Except her, yes, she is prettier when she smiles.

Captive
By
P.J. Blakey-Novis

No light in this prison. No way to determine day or night. Darkness is all I've known, literally and metaphorically, since being thrown in here. I don't know my captor, or his reasons, he simply took me one evening while I was jogging. A chloroform rag and some rope were all he needed. I feared sexual assault but there's been no contact aside from a meal tray being slid through the door twice a day. Not knowing his intentions is worse, but perhaps that's part of the plan. I can feel insanity creeping in and I know I'll never leave.

Memory Stick
By
Ryan Colley

I found a memory stick in the parking lot the other day, which I took home and plugged into my laptop. My mum always used to say, "Alan, your curiosity will be the death of you."

Anyway, the memory stick had a few random text files on there – all gibberish when I opened them. Nothing interesting. Or so I thought until the first message came through a week later.

"Do you know how computer scripts work?" the unknown sender asked simply. When I didn't answer, they replied with a photo of my front door and the text, "Knock knock, Alan."

Terra
By
Steve Stred

"This is insane."

They exited the capsule, thrusters dimming into sleep mode.

"We're the first people to stand on a new planet," Jason exclaimed, jumping to test the surface's gravitational force.

Dust bloomed and puffed in the atmosphere, little alien spores disturbed for the first time in centuries.

"Let's take it easy," Captain said, "We don't know what's in store."

They took in the landscape before them, the first eyes to stare at the distinct features. Rocks abounded, mountains visible far in the distance.

It was so enthralling they never heard Jason's cries for help until it was too late.

I
By
Timothy Friesenhahn

I am so tired of this bullshit. The world is losing its place in the universe. I need to escape this reality. This razor blade will suffice. I take the blade and slice at my own throat, laughing as the blood sprays from my arteries. This is what I wanted. As I lay bleeding out, I noticed I wasn't dying. I slashed my wrists and still, I wasn't dying. I wake up trapped inside the body the government calls A-21547. The government hears all my thoughts. Electro-therapy will find me before days end. Then I will dream of death again.

Compelled to Rise
By
Toneye Eyenot

The torchlights flickering — danse macabre; a wicked, cacophonous drumming as bodies flail and howl. Skin torn, blood flows, yet still they advance on the town. Death seeps from their eyes, relentlessly forging ahead. The dead rise, from nameless graves and family tombs. A young boy drowned... forgotten, bloated and rotten.

These necromantic merrymakers spread the cheer of endless sleep. Of nightmare realities, from which you'll never wake. The never-ending dance of doom spills through your window, fills your room. You wake too slow to realise, the life torn coldly from your eyes.

Your inert body is now compelled to rise.

Believe in Me.
By
Joe X Young

You have to believe. Belief is everything. It doesn't matter if it is religion, a magician or a personal trainer — you have to believe. What you believe, well, that's up to you. You can believe in Santa Claus, you can believe in fairies, you can even believe in the Flying Spaghetti Monster, but at the end of the day you really do have to believe. Here you are, believing that this day will lead to another one. I believe this is your last day on earth. My belief system is stronger, as is the grip on my scythe. Believe me.

The Old Man
By
Amber M. Simpson

Vanessa watched as the old man walked by her house; thin, frail and limping.

"Hello," she said cheerfully. "Would you like a drink? Something to eat?"

Without a word, the old man came over. His bloodshot eyes were crusted; gray flesh sagged off his cheeks. His breath reeked of decay as he opened his mouth, long pointed teeth poking through purple-spotted gums.

Vanessa shrieked but couldn't run as his long pink tongue shot out like a frog's, and wound around her neck. Pulled into his hungry maw quick as a wink, the old man patted his engorged belly and burped.

All Alone
By
Veronica Smith

I've locked myself up in my apartment. I can hear screaming in the streets below as the living are attacked and eaten by the dead. I watched my next door neighbor get his throat torn out yesterday and I've been here ever since. I've gone through my supplies and I figure I have enough for two weeks. Surely this couldn't last this long. Could it? At some point the dead will have eaten all the living and then what happens? I have to plan for my survival; I have to live. I only hope I won't be the only one.

Poached Egg
By
Ross Jeffery

He stumbles forward from the radiation leak. Screams until his throat gives up a bloody eruption. Clotted lumps fall from his mouth like chopped tomatoes from a can, a never-ending tide of chunks. He reaches out his arms, imploring me to help. The flesh dribbles from his extended limbs, revealing ghastly fringes of meat. I watch his eyes blister. They bubble in their sockets. He lifts a faltering hand, clasps it over one of his eyes before it succumbs. It dribbles through his fingers like a grey poached egg. He drops to the floor. Screaming. Pleading. I turn and run.

Domestic Bliss
By
J. C. Michael

She's always liked horror movies. Lights down low, an eerie soundtrack, not too much gore, but jump scares galore. So many nights we'd sit on the couch as murder and mayhem played out before us, old or new, classic or B-Movie. All harmless fun, and as the credits rolled the lights would go on, and we'd share a cuppa before bed. Turned in, we'd fall asleep in each other's arms, the nightmares done, just dreams to come. She enjoyed being scared. And now she needs to be scared of me. Because I know what the fucking bitch has been doing...

Tiny Terrors
By
Greg Bennett

Christ, not another one.

The faint scratching low on his front door was persistent. Jake had heard it before; a soft, repeating raspy sound that reminded him of his cat Harry from long ago.

The outbreak had been merciless, not just for the adults, but for children as well. Grade school and kindergarten alike, the kids were pint-sized abominations just as deadly as their adult counterparts.

Jake slid the door's small view plate open and stared at a young girl's tattered face; crushed dangling eyeball, missing jaw, a ribboned blood-stained ponytail.

He leveled his shotgun...closed his eyes...and pulled the trigger.

Slithering
By
Josh A. Murphy

It had one purpose.

It crawled, sticking to shadows, guided by moonlight.

The house was locked. It slithered through the letterbox and glided up the stairs. The crack below the bedroom door was enough to grant entry. There she slept soundly, wrapped in blankets and warm, restful slumber. Her soft snores lured it closer, soundlessly slipping below her duvet, reveling in her warmth. It expanded, its soft, boneless structure engulfing her.

She awoke, opened her mouth to scream, but was smothered by its membrane. It released its fluids.

She began to melt, sizzling, fizzling until nothing remained.

Its purpose fulfilled.

Getting Carried Away
By
Evans Light

He'd blacked out for a moment, likely from nervous anticipation.

As his surroundings snapped back into focus, Pierre found himself facedown in a pile of hay. Spitting grit, he tried to stand but his body was too heavy, as if he'd suddenly gained a thousand pounds.

He struggled once more before giving up. He didn't remember why he'd been frightened. His thoughts were wispy, ephemeral things.

The earth jolted beneath him and began to sway, rolling him over. He stared up into the blue sky, at the clouds, at two hands clutching a basket, carrying him away from the guillotine.

Asylum
By
Nerisha Kemraj

Hannah shut her eyes, avoiding the dark corner where the croaking stemmed from.

"You're not real. You're not real. They said you're not real." She rocked back and forth on the bed.

Reopening her eyes, she saw the demon standing before her; eyes glowing with rage.

She screamed as he grabbed her throat, flinging her across the room.

Grabbing her again, he smashed her head against the door, repeatedly, bloodying the tiny glass window.

He only let go when the nurses entered.

"How did she free herself? Restrain her! A third suicide attempt in three days!"

Hannah succumbed to sedation.

Fantasy
By
Regina Kenney

"Let me do yours," Megan giggled, "we did mine last night." She snuggled close to him under the covers. "It's... embarrassing," Jeff pleaded, turning a deep crimson.

He couldn't believe it had only been a month. She wasn't like any other girl he'd been with. "C'mon," she cooed, "I told you mine." He leaned in, whispering in her ear. She squealed with laughter as she put her face into the pillow. "Baby, we can totally do that."

He smiled and kissed her forehead.

Jeff reached into the nightstand drawer. Pulling out his knife, he wondered what Megan thought 'Necrophilia' meant.

Coins
By
Harris Coverley

I lie on the cool banks of the Acheron, choking, mud between my fingers, water at my heels.

I lived a virtuous and honourable life. I fought for my land, I tilled it with care, I paid my taxes, I raised strong, loyal sons for the rage of battle, and I died a good, natural death, not by my own hand or the hand of an enemy.

Yet Charon refuses to take me on his ferry without payment, the coins meant for my eyes having been lodged in my throat.

And so I lie, choking and choking, in immortal perpetuity.

New Home
By
Mark Cassell

I'd taken little notice of the other high-rise that stood between the harbour and our apartment on the seventh floor. I'd missed the first jumper; only heard the screaming onlookers. I squinted and watched the second guy plummet.

We'd moved into the neighbourhood several weeks ago and had since unpacked almost every box. I manoeuvred around the one at my feet, feeling heat rise to my face. Adrenaline or something else filled me.

From this distance, I saw their crumpled bodies on the tarmac.

Another jumper, this time from our building. Then another …

I opened the window.

I Jumped.

Cannibal
By
Dawn DeBraal

Debbie watched out the window. She was excited when a teen who was texting on his phone walked into her trap.

Snap!

The steel jaws closed on his leg. The kid screamed, writhing in pain, tried to open the jaws, but they were too overpowering.

Debbie called the others. They quickly surrounded the boy taking him inside. All the children gathered round the table anxious for the feast.

"Who wants what?" Debbie asked as she drew the knife across the stone.

"I'll take a leg!" one of the boys shouted.

"I'd love a breast, please."

"Thigh for me!" said another.

Advice
By
Valerie Lioudis

They say count the turns. If you focus on the route, you will have a better chance of telling the authorities where to find you.

They say you should feel around for the release latch. It should be somewhere near the taillights, and you can pull it if the car comes to a stop.

They say arm yourself if possible. When your captor opens the trunk, you have mere seconds to overtake them and get away.

They say all of this, and you believe it will help.

That is, until water starts pouring in and filling up the dark cavity.

Take the Long Way Home
By
Kevin Wetmore

Every night after the restaurant closes, I walk home over the Colorado Street Bridge. Yeah, the "suicide bridge."

Carla, the other server, says I'm crazy — over a hundred people have jumped to their deaths from it. It's supposed to be super haunted or something. "Don't walk across it at night," she says.

I gotta get home, don't I? I'm not suicidal. I tell her, "they don't bother me, and I don't bother them." Mostly 'cause they don't exist.

Then tonight, I felt hands on my back, throwing me over the railing.

It turns out none of the deaths were suicides.

Cinema
By
Andrew Lennon

The movie had only been playing for five minutes when I grabbed the girls head and quickly shoved it to my crotch. I'd checked that nobody was looking. Besides the old couple in the front row, it was empty. I moved her head up and down, slowly moving myself in and out of her mouth. It felt exquisite, I finished quickly. I got up from my seat and threw her head aside. It made a slight thud as it bounced off the stairs. A glance behind showed her body still sat in place. I left. The movie was rubbish anyway.

Phantom
By
RJ Meldrum

The police finally got a break; the killer's registration plate had been recorded by CCTV. The police raided his home, ready to arrest him, but it wasn't to be. The 'Right-Handed Killer' was so strong he strangled his victims with one hand. The man in front of them had no right arm, just a stump.

He smiled. Phantom limb syndrome was the name for it; a sensation his arm was still there. In his case it was a little more. He could see the ghostly outline of his arm. He could still use it. It was the perfect murder weapon.

Fiddlestyx
By
Toneye Eyenot

Lesser demon, greater demon, happy demon, cranky demon — they all just need a little love. A little… acceptance.

Fiddlestyx is a lesser demon. So 'lesser', in fact, his insignificant charm is matched only by his depressing obscurity. This makes him a cranky demon. Nobody likes a cranky demon.

People used to say "Fiddlestyx" all the time, which allowed him out of Hell for a spell and into their lives, but not so much anymore. Exclamations, like "fuck!" "shit!" etcetera grew more accepted and became the norm. Fiddlestyx has been largely forgotten, save the occasional censored curse…

But he remembers You.

Ride-Hailing
By
Ryan Colley

I love ride-hailing apps. Ordering a lift, with door to door service, without ever talking to someone? Perfect for the modern world.

When I left the nightclub and ordered my ride, I was ecstatic when it pulled up in a matter of seconds. He lowered his window and nodded, so I climbed in.

The car wasn't as clean as I was used to, but I was drunk and didn't care.

When he took a wrong turn, I assumed he was avoiding traffic. When I got a text from my ordered ride asking where I was, my blood turned to ice.

Too Little Too Late
By
Veronica Smith

The zombies shamble closer as four survivors stand back to back, weapons in their hands, with nowhere left to run. The man swings his axe, decapitating two undead at once. The woman has two machetes, one in each hand, and is stabbing as many through the face as she can. The teenage boy has a rake, which can only keep zombies off until the man or woman can turn his way and dispatch his attackers. In the middle of all three is a little girl. They will die trying to protect her although unaware that she already has been bitten.

Spectrum
By
J.C. Michael

Fresh red blood spilt under an orange sun. Home dyed hair more yellow than blonde, splayed over lush green grass as her dead eyes stare up into a clear blue sky. I purchased the dye for her, just as I had purchased the indigo denim jeans that clad her long slim legs. Purchases made this very day. The same day as I selected her, a choice based on name alone. Her name is Violet.

The rainbow is no longer the preserve of hope and pride. Now it is my symbol, and when you see it, you shall think of me.

This Little Piggy
By
Evans Light

"This Little Piggy Barbecue" was the rare overnight success among restaurant chains, locations spreading quickly from Seattle to Portland and San Francisco. The brand cornerstone was humane harvesting, and a visit to their farms revealed the happiest pigs ever seen.

The company was renowned for philanthropy, especially among the homeless. In every town where they canvassed tent cities offering work and second chances, the homeless population shrunk dramatically. As they expanded into the Denver and Phoenix markets, streets sparkled up and down the coast.

The brand could do no wrong, until a sandwich of barbecued human thumbs was accidentally served.

Afterword

Like the foreword, I'll keep this short. Thank you for reading my book. I hope you enjoyed it as much as I did. Every book I put together is basically a grouping of my favourite stories. I reject a lot, especially with the drabble books so what you are left with are the stories I loved. I don't expect everyone to have identical taste to me, but I hope I selected enough that you loved for this to have been a pleasurable ride.

If you have the time, please consider leaving a review somewhere for the book or sharing on your page. It helps more than you can know.

Thank you very much for giving up your valuable time to read something by KJK Publishing.

Kevin J. Kennedy
Editor

Printed in Great Britain
by Amazon